# *My* Embodiment *as a* Broken Record

# My Embodiment as a Broken Record

In Memory of 'The Vampire Chronicles' by Anne Rice

A Song by Maxim Nathan May 2009

Thomas-Ian Nadeau

Copyright © Thomas-Ian Nadeau.

All rights reserved. No part of this book may be reproduced in any form or by any electronic or mechanical means, including information storage and retrieval systems, without permission in writing from the publisher, except by reviewers, who may quote brief passages in a review.

ISBN:  978-1-64871-652-2   (Paperback Edition)
ISBN:  978-1-64871-654-6   (Hardcover Edition)
ISBN:  978-1-64871-651-5   (E-book Edition)

Some characters and events in this book are fictitious. Any similarity to real persons, living or dead, is coincidental and not intended by the author.

**Book Ordering Information**

Phone Number: 347-901-4929 or 347-901-4920
Email: info@globalsummithouse.com
Global Summit House
www.globalsummithouse.com

Printed in the United States of America

Whoever truly believes in my work may follow me into paradise . . . . If you truly believe after you read this you just may be a NADEAUIAN RECORDIST. I CREATED MY OWN RELIGION THAT ALL MAY FOLLOW IF THEY WANT OR YOU MAY JUST ADMIRE US, BE INDIFFERENT OR HATE US. WE WORSHIP THE GREAT GOD DANIEL AND HIS COUNTERPART MALBOWA

THIS IS BASED ON THIS BOOK YOU ARE READING RIGHT NOW . . . PLEASE JOIN US AND PLEASE DO READ THIS ENTIRE BOOK AND READ ON. THIS BOOK IS GENIUS AND IT IS GODLY . . .

## This Religion Is About Being Bisexual And Hating Bisexuals

*My Embodiment As A Broken Record questions one's morality when having done something negative as all have done at least once in their lives and the willingness to get better after a psychosis.*

*It tackles the overwhelming power it takes to go through being an innocent human drained of memories and one's love for another one dear to him/her.*

*To my loving mother and to Gaia,
the living, the self-aware, the Mother Earth...
May God be faithful...*


*In Memory of 'The Vampire Chronicles' by Anne Rice
A Song by Author Unknown
Maxim Nathan
May 2009*

*And May my Given Name be Erased,
And be Only Publishable under the name Maxim Nathan.
Later I realized I was neither gay but I was unique*

## Daniel's Embodiment

In Memory of 'The Vampire Chronicles' by Anne Rice

A Song by Maxim Nathan May 2009

The darkness has come; Malbowa the dark lord of Hell has come to destroy love and life on Earth together as they are...

# Contents

Ludicrous as a Vouch to the Devil ........................................ 1
Actuality ................................................................ 2
Reality .................................................................. 3
Episode of darkness 1 .................................................... 5
Episode of darkness 2 .................................................... 6
Episode of light redemption number 1 ..................................... 7
Episode of Light 1 ....................................................... 8
Episode of light 2 ....................................................... 9
Episode of redemption 1 ................................................. 10
Episode of Redemption 2 ................................................. 11
Exploding Final Episode 1 ............................................... 12
Solace 1 ................................................................ 15
Solace 2 ................................................................ 16
Solace 3 ................................................................ 17
Episode of Redemption 3 ................................................. 18
Final Redemption ........................................................ 19
But Forsaken once Again ................................................. 20
Alternative reason Why it didn't go Perfectly for
    Daniel and Samantha in the Heights of Heaven .......... 22
Problem Duplicity ....................................................... 26
Problem End ............................................................. 28

# Ludicrous as a Vouch to the Devil

Depending on the evil of evil men and the balance of the universe two lovers must be together once and again or die as sacrifice…

And so Malbowa is a powerful villain from the depths of Hell who has anger, Archer is a Heavenly angel who knows nothing but love who has vengeance, Samantha is a beautiful girl tainted by the loss of her right limb who has emotional struggle, and Daniel is the riveting past before Samantha's loss of limb; her one and only love who couldn't stand Samantha's deformity who is lost in finding and they all retain that first argument which is Daniel's purgatory… This is Malbowa's place on Earth.

# Actuality

Samantha who doesn't knows how to put Daniel into place in her heart thinks he still loves her… Although Daniel has totally forgotten about Samantha because she is deformed the demon Malbowa is controlling his every desire to have her once again even though he is unloving… Through darkness Malbowa takes Daniel's spirit.

It seems Daniel loved Samantha for being perfect because he is imperfect and things won't work anymore until Samantha is cured until then in his heart Daniel is possessed and doesn't sees Samantha for the loving caring girl that she is anymore… Through darkness and light Daniel is a man of glory.

Archer the sole angel cast down from the Heavens must choose between life and death if Samantha does not have her rightful place in Heaven; if Samantha finds her place in Heaven this may reset the balance in Heaven, Hell, or on Earth for the love Daniel and Samantha shared would then take place in the afterlife and things would smoothen over… If Daniel learns the true notion of love he may find his place in Heaven one day, but for now he is condemned for having destroyed balance in Heaven, Hell, or on Earth… I hope Daniel will be okay on his journey through the bold Earth.

# Reality

The love Daniel and Samantha shared kept the realms together. If Daniel were pure at heart Samantha's sudden imperfection would not be a cause for abandonment… Their love therefore is a supposed fixed point in time that has been broken…

Destruction may be the path if Heaven does nothing to the likes of Hell who desires false love as a way to claim the Earth and Heaven… Putting aside all other disasters which will happen without love this is not actually love and is a thing to be reckoned with…Malbowa still remains king of the overwhelming sun and beneath that the underworld, what will happen next?

But should love be a fixed point in time? Love is not meant, love is what we make of it at least for us as human beings… So it shouldn't be for it would have to work in every circumstance as long as two lovers live and human beings don't live forever nor are they perfect. (So this story could be called a good example of eternal life and just regular love.) Shame is lethal for Daniel the man of dream to be part of such a chaotic fixation over Samantha

Since things are already settled and the universe might as well fall into the pits of Hell Samantha and Daniel must wait because the sun may burst but then again Samantha may get her aim and two human lovers may be together once again…

True everlasting love mainly only belongs to gods and angels because their bodies do not break in shape or form, And so a possessed Daniel will seek out Samantha no matter what it takes.

# Episode of darkness 1

A darkness has erupted many have died Archer the sole angel bound to Earth must choose between saving Earth or casting

Heaven into a new eternal light… Choosing Earth Archer finds solemn friends in mankind's world. Stripped of his wings he must choose between life and death to save a young girl from desecration and give her rightful place in Heaven… If he survives the task to which is at hand he will be given his rightful place in Heaven and his peer angels watch upon him from the heights of Heaven.

*I was insane...*

# Episode of darkness 2

Together with his villains Malbowa has decided to throw away the works God had formulated for him and start a new age and whatever it takes Daniel will be there under strict rule of Malbowa the Devil.

# Episode of light redemption number 1

The age of man is in blossom thanks to Archer's sacrifice of Heaven's sanctity but can Malbowa use the given light that shines from the sun that Heaven wanted so badly from themselves to his advantage and turn Earth into a chaotic sphere full of fi re??? The gods on planet Earth devised by other religions wilt sorrow, pity, and anger from the Hell demon Malbowa. Connected now is all religion created by man…

Whatever; whatever the gods say, it is not that important, but they may rule the world once Malbowa fails his conquest.

*I am now Malbowa…*

# Episode of Light 1

A short cut through the age of gold tells of a sculptor who knows no pain when dealing with the deceased. Malbowa's tortures of the human race has gone on for centuries. Can light be turned and create a new age where the sculptor can turn Malbowa into a gentle giant? Even though the sculptor being the last remanence of his kind holding only the key to the chamber which fabricated the gods or will the conviction of the gods passed on into another world remain forever. Now that the gods and angels have both been created as real by Daniel and Samantha, 'nothing can be real.' Nor can Daniel keep his head up high under a sun so clear and evil.

*Daniel is also I vs. myself the Devil*

# Episode of light 2

Reluctant sacrifice has been made through Heaven and in Hell. Th e arch angel Archer sacrificed his wings to grow arms and legs of man. Malbowa has sacrificed the ties of Heaven, and through Heaven a young girl bound still to Earth mutilated in a chain saw accident has grown a love and lost. Can she decide her truest desires? On Earth her lover Daniel before her deformity, in Heaven the yearning for paradise, and in Hell the desire to suffer forever for in acceptance of all her losses including a tainted destiny to have Daniel a husband and his child? All these things are tied together; can past and fate hold all these things together??? Samantha is the key... A beautiful woman and a beautiful Lamb... *and boy did I love Samantha...*

# Episode of redemption 1

Dreams are made through sunken towers; evil fi ends have desecrated the gods, what fi re that once delivered Heaven a light filled with joy has become unwelcoming… The fi ends have travelled to Heavens and have rested and bathed in the eternal springs once so populated by the given angels… Through mercy of the Heavens it commands new fate… On Earth, in Heaven, or deep within the core of the Earth; Hell an unknown guided darkness inspires and is yearned by Malbowa the dark lord of Hell… Archer unites Malbowa into a strange void filled with laughter… What once was God for both of them has become a riveting past cast down from the Heavens… Archer walking on both feet unable to fly back into the sky where he came from decides to enchant Malbowa with this guided not so darkness… And will homosexuality be the end of this time.]

# Episode of Redemption 2

His plans on middle Earth are simple retrieve Samantha's life alone or in the darkness of regret or a second encounter with the fated loss of her once true lover Daniel now beckoned by the Heavens…

Malbowa accepts the darkness's path and twines to give a second face to face of the once lovers Daniel the conceited and Samantha the loving but bitter fateful…Please God save Daniel from O merciless Hell.

# Exploding Final Episode 1

Alleged power of the dark lord absorbs Daniel into believing he has lost his conviction in God… Wondering why he deserted Samantha those many years ago has become unwelcoming…

Pledged to find God again and bring back light into a hole filled with stubbornness Daniel will seek out Samantha in the meadows of the farms where she grew up and still resides…

Contemplating the darkness Malbowa has a hand to play in all these occasions for foreplay knowing that Daniel's true nature has repulsed the very idea of Samantha he must meddle to bring the sun upon the Earth's crust and fabricate these two lovers in his dominion with all the rest of the spilt over juice of Heaven's reluctance to take in more than in its share of man who has sinned in one way or another… Daniel leaps over the broken torn fences of the farm. Having arrived from his vehicle the sky looked strangely lifeless and dead; not to mention the dark sky clouded over head; leaving his vehicle behind Daniel finds Samantha all alone in her misery across the fence; lurking through she sees him and before she can react Daniel plainly asks her what had happened; she responds, "From the west monsters of all varieties came through the meadows and upon the crops closer still to our home and when arrived grabbed my father, mother, and brother flying themselves back into the soils of the Earth; my family included. All spoils included my family and my lover has gone into the abyss... Can light be cast and bring back Daniel my fated someone or will I always live in grieve of loving him? Does he not see that half a dozen limbs are as good as one should have?"

Light shines and Daniel's possession seams to fade away realizing who is before he dwells deeper into his heart for the answers to tell but finds nothing.

"Can what was once Samantha stream grass and daises of bed flowers or through this edge do things find heart???"

Opens a portal and all seams calm then steps out the demon Malbowa in deep despair, "You haven't spoken the truth have you? From your heart??? Does Darkness bathed with light bring back memories of past fates of former times or does it allow them to reconcile themselves into better happenings??? I will not allow this. Come into my dominion Daniel and will shall fi x the Earth's crust so that your desire for Samantha shall fade and what fate Samantha has all shall fade... I am your man Daniel... Be pretty with me if you can."

Everything disappears... Light and Hell all formed Daniel is all alone chained to the likes of a stone wall all alone in a red heated glowing darkness and only the faint whisper of torch fire can be heard.

Where there is darkness there is always light because Daniel is not alone; Malbowa is there and Malbowa cares for Daniel's face especially, so he won't hurt him as badly as he might have if he was ugly... And sure Daniel goes to bed with a deranged former angel without his own choice.

# Solace 1

Meanwhile Archer transports the grieved Samantha back into the heights of Heaven where she is awarded back her right limb. Archer finds solace in the heights of Heaven and is favoured over the given light lost from Heaven onto Earth… Daniel is Malbowa's personal dominion for he challenged the depths of Hell to a stronger notion of love… All that seems plausible is that Daniel stays in Hell and Samantha is awarded back her lost right limb… Th e balance is set indefinitely and what love Samantha had for Daniel is changed forever… This is what you call putting to rest a fatal wound otherwise life threatening and so can light be shone and bring back the once true lovers Daniel the conceited and Samantha the loving but bitter fateful or will the conviction of the gods passed on into another world remain forever???

Daniel where are you where have you gone?
*creative writing makes its way from fiction to reality…*

## Solace 2

Ten thousand years have passed in Hell and only thirty on Earth and in Heaven since things do move slowly in Hell? Daniel resides that fate will no longer allow his living body to appear back on Earth for he damned and dead? He wishes to make up for his conceitedness towards Samantha? Daniel wishes to offer his now pure soul to the Devil in return for eternal life on Earth where he senses Samantha resides now??? "Without a soul…", the Devil replies, "And it being owned by the Devil I can only grant you a life time on Earth where it is almost certain you shall never find Samantha and there not being able to repent for your sinfulness towards her for she now resides in Heaven…

What I can offer you is this… Eternal life in Heaven, Hell, and on Earth??? You will be my minion until the end of time, but you may see Samantha once in this time as a chance to repent and express your new found understanding of love…" And we almost forgot Daniel's soulless body.

## Solace 3

Thirty years have passed in Heaven and on Earth. What once was the grieved Samantha is now a blossoming flower... Having lost her family and Daniel she now finds hope in reincarnation where she may forget and live another life entirely. She asks God and God replies, "Sorry your place is here... What I can do for you is make you an angel. Forget about the past and walk with me..."

# Episode of Redemption 3

The lovers after infinity of years meet; Samantha a full pledged angel and Daniel a guided spirit without a soul… Samantha lingers and says, "I have forgotten about you…" Daniel replies,

"And I a soulless but ever aged spirit for things do move slowly in all realms have decided that I cannot be without your delicate essence from the day you were born…" I pledge that this day is my last that I will never see you once more. "I pledge that I vow to become a man once again and live another lifetime on Earth with you as my angel…" How could Daniel find his heart without a soul.

# Final Redemption

And so God would not let Samantha give up her angelic body for sake of the balance of the stars, but proposes that she guide Daniel through his passage on Earth into Heaven where they may one day both be angels and lovers once more...

# But Forsaken once Again

The passage was good in Heaven, Hell, or on Earth and not

'And' because they all happened separately especially when Daniel's soul was owned by the Devil and he lingered in all realms? What, Earth and Daniel's soul were granted back so the end of time is no longer?

The realm of angels welcomed Daniel who had been through so much to reach the Heavens and Daniel knew that Samantha was proposed to reach the Heavens so early in her life because of his deeds and how their love if any has a great effect over the balance of all realms and that it is wished that their love be held in a working balanced dominion where they are honourable lovers… So forth God welcomes back the gods from a hidden paradise to wed Daniel and Samantha in a cathedral of Heaven… It was said that by fate depending on the outcome of Daniel's purity and Samantha's everlasting love that Daniel and Samantha would reunite in Heaven, Hell, or on Earth, but spend many years apart in Heaven and in Hell as atonement to the universe, because their love broken or unbroken was said to be so pure that it held a miraculous temperament over time and Daniel and Samantha must always be fateful or disaster may happen once more and this time it may never cease in Heaven, Hell, or on Earth; for what would happen if a fixed point in time were broken in the afterlife???

Chaos to love as a fixed point in time and if it serves your happiness we'll live forever re-finding our hearts for what true love was and what it was not...

It is the memory of the love that we shared that is eternal. O and Daniel's love was not eternal until now. Daniel's memory of the real Samantha was stored away in his heart because he could stand the decrepit state she was in... Now that Daniel remembers the woman he loved so very much and why he did the universe may come back together and Daniel may have been able to reunite with Samantha in Heaven, Hell or on Earth to truly understand that Samantha was beautiful all along...

The truth is Daniel got beaten to a bloody pulp by Malbowa the dark lord of Hell and there removing Daniel of his innocence so Samantha couldn't love him properly anymore and now Malbowa realizes that physical beatings don't have to be all that great at all; he having misunderstood Daniel's life story and aim. Malbowa had wished so much to destroy the universe with an incredibly stupid fixed point in time that he had designed...

For homosexuality's sake I hope this story is just a story. *but I was homosexual, I was bi-sexual*

# Alternative reason Why it didn't go Perfectly for Daniel and Samantha in the Heights of Heaven

Before Daniel met the actual Samantha he knew those many years ago Daniel was once a good person but mutated through lives eternal grieve... He met Samantha and all was well until Samantha started grieving herself... And so Daniel pointed the finger at Samantha's lost marvellous beauty in vain and in shame and was condemned to purgatory, and later on to Hell... And purgatory once again... Archer the satanic but silenced angel was given back his youth through Daniel's abomination and was tasked by the elements and God to bring tranquillity back to the universe through satanic rituals... So forth he welcomed Malbowa into a strange void filled with laughter so that Malbowa would one day bring Daniel to Hell, and purgatory...

The Goddess Samantha was removed of her goddess powers through mutilation, and Daniel no longer desired his chosen once beautiful wife... Daniel was condemned for abandoning his goddess wife... And was made monotheist; condemned to Earth, Heaven, and Hell; Daniel was later condemned to purgatory and later on to Hell, and purgatory once again. Samantha was made an angel with the power to seduce the memories of man once she met their hateful selves And boy was she good... *no longer can I be gay I must be myself*

Daniel had five children; one was cool, three were vibrant, and one was a womaniser...Condemned to the Earth for reinitiating his long lost relationship with his ex-wife Rebecca and there having children with her; Daniel chose solitude over madness and was deserted by angels and Heaven to realize the beauty of this very woman he was not especially fond of at the beginning; Samantha... Daniel is not a fool but was abused by those kinds of people so he must lurk in the darkness and in the light and persuade woman to do as he may... He found Samantha and was seduced by her eternal beauty and Tranquility and deep in his heart he knew he would never be with another woman but her ever again... And the drag is Daniel has changed. Malbowa has screwed with Daniel's memories and future destinies for another chaos on Earth.

Condemned to the ocean for his former relationship with his ex-wife... Daniel knows that he has very little emotion and self pity and chooses to learn from Samantha's massive compassionate self...

He asked Samantha... "One day I once hated all children of man, I wanted some to be happy and others to pay for their insanity. Does that make me a bad person???"

Samantha replied, "Yes it does but you are not bad anymore while you are with me..."

"I beg to defer", replied Daniel, "It is the boldness of man that is evil, 'not me'. I wish everybody the best that God can give...

And you will pay for your raft towards me through God's hands... My Family made me leave that ex-wife of mine and me also for your own well being... Entitle gravity cut off cut off the goddess Samantha's right arm and condemns me to purgatory and Hell and both of us one day to Heaven..."

*and Daniel never committed the crime in the first place*

It was done through the elements and nothing was ever the same in Heaven, Hell, or on Earth. Both forgot the incident and Daniel came to realize he was always a good person after his purgatory but the rest is up to God if he will ever be viewed as a good person and if the Earth will ever accept him for abandoning the actual Samantha those many years ago, but that is another story entirely because it is a lifelong dream that we can be accepted by God and man alike, but that will never happen because of ignorant people who cannot understand a man of enlightened self... Th e end... Not even. Ugliness could not be stood by Daniel the man of dreams... Tis' the story of our first true loves... The woman you've been related to a good part of your life and whom you trust because she is understood and trustworthy... Daniel was somehow related to Samantha's loss of limb... Daniel was so insulted by Samantha's put down towards his temporarily renewed relationship with his ex-wife while they were dating that he wished ill fate upon her and it happened... Daniel and Samantha then parted ways towards another world and this world is purely surreal because Daniel is a failed super hero who doesn't care about helping others anymore because he doesn't have time... Daniel goes to the movies a lot, smokes pot and drinks licker... Man versus self in its most simplistic of forms. How could Malbowa be so stupid and create love as a fixed point in time? Malbowa must suffer from major disorganization problems as God is his judge and the universe may come back together from the depths of Heaven...

*let it be said that for me the Devil is not real*

"You're love is unconditional and so forth you're in my heart always Samantha and May the rain swallow us whole Samantha." elaborates Daniel after putting himself back together... No names for the wicked possessed by Devils.

## Problem Duplicity

Daniel Has Schizophrenia... Daniel was diagnosed in 2003, Daniel is Sam McGee from the Cremation of Sam McGee 'Me'

...Sam has Paranoid Schizophrenia... Schizophrenia talking to Sam, Paranoid Schizophrenia talking to Daniel; they wrote this as Disorganized Schizophrenia... This is how Paranoid Schizophrenia writes a story: he writes it as Disorganized Schizophrenia but it's actually Schizophrenia he likes the most...

Mix them together and they'll probably talk and come to a conclusion... The Bearded Lady Disease... Th is was a promotion for the Bearded Lady Disease...:

When you're living in the slums and the drug's not enough...

Drink licker, smoke pot, and get out of my face dumb bum 'cum'...

Whenever you're living in the slums and there are nibbles in your cup; get out of my room dumb bum 'pot'...

Whenever you're living in the slums and there's licker in your bum smoke pot dumb bum 'what?'...

Whenever you're living in the slums and the drug's getting in your hum get sucked dumb bum 'pot'...

And whenever you're living in the slums and the Devil is getting in your bum get out of my house dumb bum 'what?'...

> Or stay inside forever dumb bum 'what?'...
> And get in my house dumb bum 'hot'...
> Or neither nor dumb bum 'what?'...
> Because that's okay dumb bum 'what?'...
> I'll be alone dumb bum hotter than 'what?'...

And get some well deserved shut eye that I've been missing for a while and that also without you or righteous beauty and the highs that I truly desire and the guilt that I feel for you...

Best wishes to all you mother fuckers with a dumb bum 'what?' diary of forbidden dreams... Th e Devil with his dark evil magic made Daniel into a revolting bisexual.

# Problem End

Refer to 'Schizophrenia: The Bearded Lady Disease' by J. Michael Mahoney published in 2006 if you want to truly understand the severe bisexual conflict that is the bearded lady disease and syndrome... By actuality Daniel was bisexual. When he was younger he suffered from severe bisexual conflict because he did not want to be homosexual and others to think he was satanic and ridicule him. Always having been interested in woman he was fully capable of being heterosexual and climbed over to that side of the fence...

In later years having been diagnosed with Schizophrenia he read the book 'Schizophrenia: The Bearded Lady Disease' by J. Michael Mahoney and wanted to share his new found understanding of his disorder that he and others like him also might be beneficial to share with their ex-wives if they had one but in Daniel's case things between him and his ex-wife got more complicated and a secret bunch of children arose; he and her having fallen back in love that was not too serious but was something... It was the spur of the moment and it brewed Quintuplets and so Samantha found out about those Quintuplets and Daniel was forced to break everything off with his ex-wife so that he could remain in a relationship with Samantha because he was more in love with her than anything else, but Samantha couldn't always handle the fact that Daniel still had feelings for his ex-wife and had cheated on her so they got into an argument, feelings spurred and Daniel wished ill fate upon Samantha and it happened through the demon of fate Chronos the Time; crow and Daniel left her through the demon of temptation Diablo through fate of God after having stopped to take his medication and was persuaded by the Devil to go back and taunt Samantha for his own well being alone in the darkness of Jesus Christ where God spoke out of that darkness; take your medication...

But this is all crazy. This is only what the Devil makes Daniel remember. Daniel was once an honest and proud man who loved women as ever, but Malbowa wants Daniel and his personal demons to destroy him since he wants his love as a fixed point in time to destroy the world for his personal control.

<u>The End</u>

www.ingramcontent.com/pod-product-compliance
Lightning Source LLC
LaVergne TN
LVHW041551060526
838200LV00037B/1242